W9-DCJ-516

EDITH & MR. BEAR

DARE WRIGHT

Houghton Mifflin Company

Boston

To my generous and loving voluntary Godmother

The text of this book is set in 17-point Bodoni Book.

Originally published by Random House, Inc.

This title was originally cataloged by the Library of Congress as follows:
Wright, Dare. Edith & Mr. Bear.
1 v. (unpaged) illus. 33 cm.
I. Title. PZ7.W935Ed   64-20565
RNF ISBN: 0-618-00332-0 PAP ISBN: 0-618-04253-9

Manufactured in the United States of America
LBM 10 9 8 7 6 5 4

At the foot of the stairs, where they could watch the front door, sat Edith and Little Bear.

They were waiting for Mr. Bear to come home from a trip.

"I wish that he'd hurry up and get here," said Little Bear.

"Be quiet, Little Bear. I'm reading to you," said Edith.

"I wonder if Mr. Bear will bring us a present," said
Little Bear.
"Of course he will," Edith said. "He always does."
Just then the front door opened, and on the threshold
stood Mr. Bear with his luggage and a large package.
Little Bear nudged Edith. "Look, it's a big present!"
he said.
But the package wasn't for them.

There *were* presents for them — a sailboat for Little Bear
and a party dress for Edith.
"Oh, Mr. Bear, it's a long dress! Oh, thank you. Look,
Little Bear, I have a long dress," cried Edith.
"My sailboat's better than a silly dress," said Little Bear.

Edith couldn't wait to put on her dress.

"Do hurry with the buttons, Mr. Bear," she begged.

"I want to see how I look."

Little Bear couldn't wait to try out his sailboat.

"Now it's my turn," said Mr. Bear, cutting the string of the mysterious big package.

"Please, Mr. Bear, what's in it?" asked Edith.

"Just wait and see," said Mr. Bear.

"Come on back, Little Bear. Mr. Bear is going to open his parcel now," called Edith.

"Look out, Little Bear,"
said Edith. "Your old boat
is dripping all over my
new dress."
But she forgot all about her
dress when Mr. Bear got the
package open.
Inside was a clock.
Edith had never seen such
a clock.
The sides were made of
glass. You could see the
pendulum swing, and watch
the wheels go round.

"This is a present for me," said Mr. Bear.

"Who gave it to you?" asked Little Bear.

"I gave it to myself," said Mr. Bear.

"Where are you going to put it?" asked Edith.

"On the mantel," said Mr. Bear.

"But that's so high up," said Edith. "We won't be able to see the wheels go round."

"It'll be safe there," said Mr. Bear.

And that's where the clock went — right in the middle
of the high mantelpiece.
Edith was always stopping to stare up at it. She loved
to hear the hours chime, and to watch the slow swing of
the pendulum.
"I wish I could touch it, Kitten," said Edith.

So one day when she
was alone Edith built
a stairway of chairs and
books, and climbed
up to where she could
touch the clock.

She turned it around, opened the back, and put
her hand in.
When she touched the pendulum, it stopped.
Edith snatched her hand out so fast that she lost
her balance.

She teetered on the pile of books, grabbed at the clock
to save herself, and down with a crash came Edith and
the clock together.
Edith wasn't hurt.

But nothing was left of the clock except broken glass
and wheels that didn't go round.
All Edith could think of was how to hide the dreadful
thing that she had done.
As fast as she could, she put away the books.

She took a mop, and swept the bits of clock under the
logs in the fireplace.
Then she ran and hid in her room.
"Maybe Mr. Bear won't notice right away," she thought.

But Mr. Bear noticed!

"Edith! Little Bear! Come here at once," he roared.

"Which of you broke this clock?"

"I didn't," said Little Bear.

Edith opened her mouth to say "I did it," but the words
didn't come. She shook her head.

"Very well," said Mr. Bear, gathering up the broken
pieces, "but whichever one of you is lying isn't going
to be very happy. You're sure you didn't do it, Edith?"

Edith looked away. She swallowed. "I didn't do it,"
she said.

Mr. Bear was right. From then on Edith wasn't a bit happy.

She didn't feel like playing with Little Bear.

She couldn't keep her mind on her lessons.

"Two and two don't make five, stupid," said Little Bear.

"I know," said Edith. "I was thinking about something

else." What she was thinking about was the clock.

She didn't even enjoy her birthday party, although she
wore her new dress and had a cake with candles.
"Oh, Kitten," she said, "you're the only one I can tell.
I broke the clock, and if he knew it Mr. Bear would
never have given me a birthday party at all. He'd hate
me. Everybody would hate me."

She quarreled with Little
Bear.
"What do you think of my
painting, Little Bear?" she
asked.
"It needs more orange," said
Little Bear.
"It does not!" said Edith.
She stepped back to look,
and kicked over a paint pot.

"You've ruined my drawing,"
howled Little Bear.
"You did it yourself, and you
can't draw anyway," said
Edith, and she slapped him.
"I don't like you. You're
horrid," shouted Little Bear.
"I never want to play with
you again!"

"It was all my fault," thought Edith, when Little Bear had rushed away, clutching his spoiled drawing. "I *am* horrid. I get horrider every day. Pretty soon nobody will like me. Maybe I should run away."

The more Edith thought about it the better the idea seemed.

"I'll go right now," she decided.

She changed into her outdoor clothes.

She stole quietly out of the house.

She ran and ran, and soon the streets around her were
all unfamiliar.

She fell and skinned her knee.

Lunchtime came, and there was nothing for her to eat.

She was tired and cold. She cried herself to sleep beside
an ash can, and woke wondering where she was.

When Edith was missing
at lunch Mr. Bear began
calling all the neighbors.
No one had seen Edith.

"She was mean to me this
morning, and I got mad
at her. I haven't seen her
since. I'm sorry, Mr. Bear,"
said Little Bear.

"There, there," said Mr.
Bear, although he was
really very worried. "I'm
sure she's all right."

"Who are you going to call now?" asked Little Bear.
"The police. They'll soon find her. She must be near
by," said Mr. Bear.

But Edith wasn't near by. She had gone on until she came to a great river lined with piers. At one pier a ship was getting ready to sail.

It was a very big ship indeed. "It's so big that it must be going far away," thought Edith. "If I could sneak on board it would take me far away, too, and I would never, never have to tell Mr. Bear that I was the one who broke his clock."

Then she thought that never, never would she see
Mr. Bear and Little Bear again!
She burst into tears.
"I want to go home," she cried.

But how could she go home?
"I could if I told Mr. Bear the truth about the clock,"
thought Edith.
So she dried her tears and set out for home.

Dusk was beginning to fall before Edith found her own
street again.

The house door stood ajar, and she crept in.

Mr. Bear was pacing anxiously up and down the living
room, with Little Bear at his heels, when a bedraggled
little figure appeared in the doorway.

"I've come home," said Edith, "and, Mr. Bear, there's
something I have to tell you."

"Now, now, no talking until we get you warm and clean
you up. You're a mess, Edith. Wherever have you been?
We've been frantic," said Mr. Bear.

He popped her right into the bathtub.

"Lots of soap, Edith, and scrub hard," said Mr. Bear.

"But I have to talk to you," said Edith.

"All in good time," said Mr. Bear, drying her.

"But, Mr. Bear, I have to tell you now."

"Hot milk next," said Mr. Bear.

"I can't drink it. Not until I tell you," said Edith. "Oh, Mr. Bear, I did it. I broke your clock. And now you won't love me any more."

"Well, now, I always thought it was you. I've been waiting for you to tell me. Why did you lie about it, Edith?" asked Mr. Bear.

"I loved the clock so much. I never meant to hurt it. I only wanted to touch it, and I broke it all to pieces. I just couldn't tell you," said Edith.

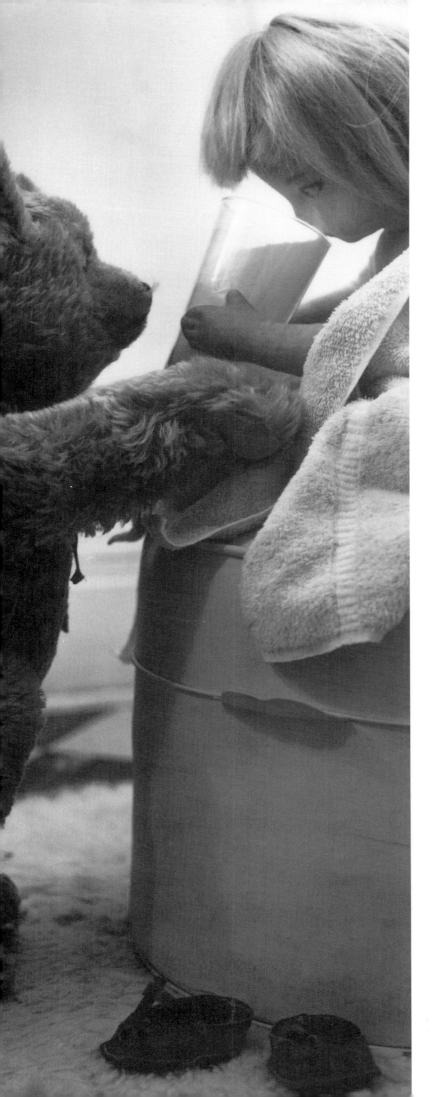

"It was naughty of you
to touch the clock without
asking me, Edith, but I
know you didn't break it
on purpose. I wouldn't
have punished you for an
accident. If only you had
told me the truth," said
Mr. Bear.

"I wish I had," said Edith.

"And you were very unfair to Little Bear. What if I had blamed him for it?" asked Mr. Bear.

"I know," said Edith. "How are you going to punish me?"

"I'm not. I think you've already punished yourself," said Mr. Bear.

"I'd feel better if you punished me," said Edith.

"I know you would," said Mr. Bear, "but I believe you've learned your lesson. I don't think you'll lie again. Now into bed with you."

"Oh, Mr. Bear, I do feel so much better," said Edith as Mr. Bear tucked her in. "You don't hate me — really and truly?"

"Don't be foolish, Edith. Of course I don't hate you," answered Mr. Bear. "Go to sleep."

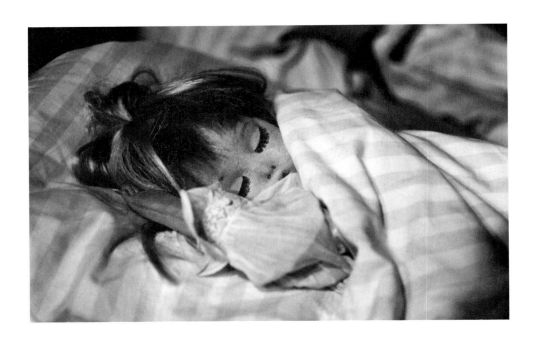

Edith went to sleep happy.

And she woke up happy.

"Oh, Mr. Bear, everything is so nice today. I love
everybody," Edith cried.

"All right, but be careful of my glasses," said Mr. Bear.

"I love you most of all, dear Mr. Bear," said Edith.

"Thank you," said Mr. Bear, "but don't choke me, Edith."

"Don't ever tell a lie, Little Bear," said Edith.

"I didn't," said Little Bear.

"I'll never do anything bad again," said Edith.

"H-m-m," said Mr. Bear.

"I'll be good forever and ever," insisted Edith.

Of course she wasn't!

She and Little Bear got into all kinds of mischief.
There was the time that Edith suggested digging up the
daffodil bulbs which Mr. Bear had just planted. She
wanted to see if they had begun to grow yet.
They hadn't, and Edith and Little Bear quickly planted
them all again — upside down!
"I can't understand why those daffodils never came up,"
said Mr. Bear in the spring.

There was the time Edith decided to cook a surprise
for Mr. Bear.

"You're making an awful mess," said Little Bear.

"All good cooks make messes," Edith said. "Hand me
the salt, Little Bear, and then we'll light the stove."

"All right, but you know what Mr. Bear has told us
about using matches," said Little Bear.

"I can't cook without a fire," said Edith.

"I just hope Mr. Bear doesn't catch us," said Little Bear. Mr. Bear did catch them! He turned them both over his knee right then and there. "You might have burned down the whole house with us in it," growled Mr. Bear. "Don't ever dare touch matches again!"

There were all the times that Edith boasted about her adventures the day she had run away.

"Little Bear, did I ever tell you about sleeping beside the ash can all by myself?" asked Edith as they were walking through the park one day.

"Only about a hundred times," said Little Bear. "Let's sail my boat."

"That's only a toy boat. You've never seen a real boat like the huge one that I was on the time I was going to sail far away all by myself," said Edith.

"Edith," said Mr. Bear, "what was that you said about being on a boat?"

"Well, the boat I thought about getting on," corrected Edith quickly, because never again did she tell Mr. Bear a lie.